HEAVEN, TEA & SWEET POTATO PIE

Heaven, Tea & Sweet Potato Pie

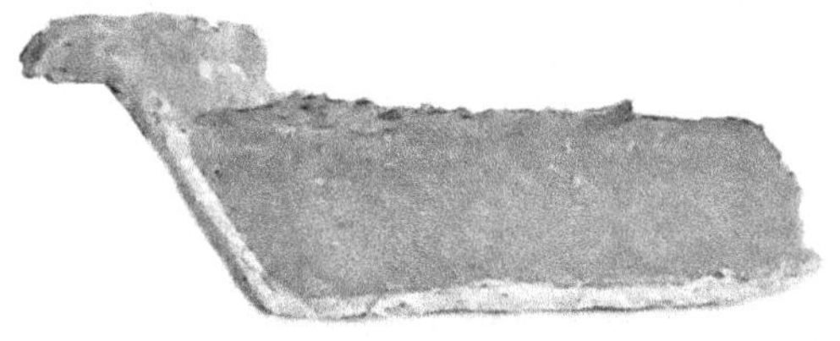

A LORD TOPH Book

Monté CrisToph Literature Copyright © 2020

ISBN: 9781655817588

CONTENTS

DEDICATION

In Loving memory of my dear mother, aunts & uncle

HEAVEN, TEA & SWEET POTATO PIE

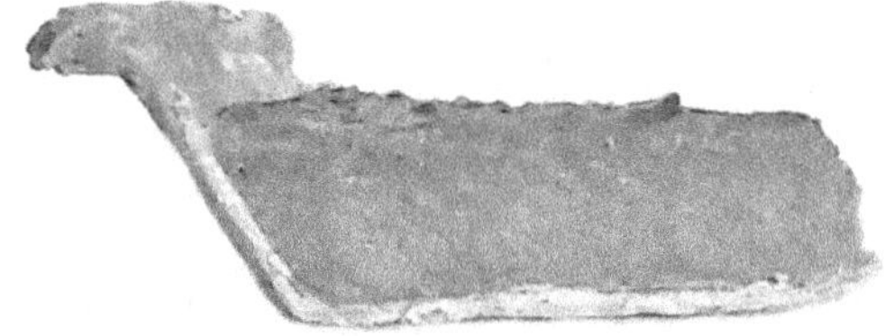

I arrived there nearly miraculously, due to heavy indigestion

and when my heart decided to momentarily stall. But once I

got there, to my surprise I realized, it was indeed by Divine

intention and was hardly any miracle at all.

My soul had seemingly absconded from body and had willingly

ascended quite peacefully and ethereally. Then I, in some

surreal form of consciousness arrived weightlessly in a space, moreover a special place, which was exactly where I had long

before promised to one day be.

As my sight began to slowly focus in on what I speculated

before me to be a sole, sitting solemn figure. It was quickly

confirmed by unforgettable gestures and subtle movements

within this saintly embodiment of a particular person that I

have my entire life cherished… My, what a glorious picture!

****

There she was and there I was, witnessing her calm and in

perfect contentment – Splendid again in all her youth. She was

sitting while tending to a simple, yet immaculately dressed little table presented with her best silverware, tea set, fine China and one of her crystal bowls filled with an abundance of fresh fruit.

Upon looking up at me with the most, sincere benignity, which I so dearly remember her possessing, she gave an endearing nod as a silent invitation for me to sit down and join her in a blessing.

I did so and in doing so, my eyes welled up with tears as my arms began to feel the sensation of intense horripilation.

Merely hearing the modest, tender tone of her voice again after all these years was to me nothing less than a joyous appreciation.

With head humbly bowed, I joined her in saying grace and giving thanks to the heavenly father for the blessings, food and nourishment which we were about to receive. Once this was done, we both slowly lifted our heads, she then smiled and began to softly speak to me.

"I am so grateful and very glad to see you little boy," which is what she called me well into my adulthood. It was her pet name which she had lovingly given me and would never fail to call me, just as she had told me she always would.

****

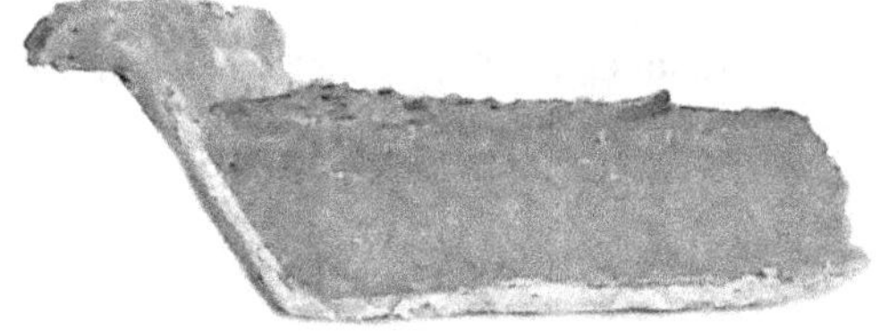

I, the man who joined her and sat before her, had aged so much from the time she was healthy, sound and alive. Yet as an elder of a respected past, she would always envision me being bright and youthful in her eyes.

"Aunt Minnie" I said impulsively as if it were some faint effort just to see how she would respond… Respond in the same way she had before on the earthly plane, now that she was existing celestially beyond. Then warmly and affectionately, "Yes, little boy?" was how she casually replied as she proceeded to pour the tea. This made me grin a grin which I hadn't since my tender youth and she in turn, smiled happily back at me.

It was the most benevolent, loving kind of smile – The kind that puts one's soul at ease. Here in this arcadian realm of other-life, it was unquestionably apparent she was totally at peace.

From the clearest yellows to the most vivid reds and the deepest blues, a multitude of calming hues bled out around us. If I had been unsure of what this place was before, I was now certain where I was.

"It's so beautiful to see it every day… It truly is a blessing, dear!" she said in response to my intrigue. I was in wonderment as I sat observing the brilliant colors in all their magnificence as she carefully poured us tea.

Then suddenly I noticed, a rich aroma which blissfully and instantly filled the air. It was kin to a smell from my fondest memories, when life for me was innocent, pure and fair. "I'd know that smell anywhere!" I thought to myself as the smell became pleasingly more intense. It was as distinct as any favored herb or flower, be it verbena or frankincense. Comforting and warm, the delightfully buttery redolence had always been. With its wonderous accompaniment of cinnamon, brown sugar, nutmeg and vanilla, pleasant times of my past were ignited once again.

Aunt Minnie smiled as I began to inquire, as though she had anticipated or expected. Then of course, I uttered my query, which was just as she had suspected.

"Is that sweet potato pie I'm smelling, Aunt Minnie?" I asked in surprise as she handed me my cup of tea. "It sure is, baby" she said as she chuckled in contentment, "I figured we'd have a little bite of something sweet."

There was no stove, no oven I could see, at least none to my recollection. But as the irresistible fragrance drew nearer, I knew it had undoubtedly been prepared to perfection.

****

And suddenly I noticed, from a lone, billowing cloud, silhouettes began to gradually manifest. I had no earthly idea what it was or was coming to be, yet with curiosity I looked on eagerly to witness.

Aunt Minnie observed my anxious gaze as though she were appeased by it, as the silhouettes subtly and mystifyingly took form. It was indeed a miracle for my eyes to see yet here, it seemed an instance of the norm.

Things come in threes I have been told and have amusingly thought for as long as I can remember. Yet the three images which solidified from the mist of the cloud, would be impossible for any man to render.

In sheer amazement I sat stupefied as I watched these heavenly beings approach me. With beautifully bright, uplifting smiles, they appeared to be coming to join Aunt Minnie and me for tea. These were souls which had been called home, so to say, long before Aunt Minnie had ever journeyed on from earth. They had all watched over and cared for me ever since my birth.

Absolutely – I was overwhelmed and realistically, humanly in disbelief. I simply could not equate or begin to fathom how any of this could actually be. "Here I am" I thought, "Sitting and having tea with my dear Aunt Minnie. Yet now as far as blessings, wants and wishes go, it appears I have been given a plenty!"

A constant stream of tears began to roll down my cheeks, as I did my best to wipe my eyes. Coming towards me were my Aunt Zerita on the left, with my Uncle Calvin on the right and in the middle was my loving mother, holding the freshly made sweet potato pie.

"You know your Aunt Minnie, she only bakes cakes" Aunt Minnie commented in third person, much like she always did before. "So, I thought it would be best to get your mother to make it and bring it over," she added as Mother, Uncle Calvin and Aunt Zerita revealed what else was in store.

Uncle Calvin then placed a bunch of old letters and photos on the table, in the place where he was to sit. Aunt Zerita gently sat down a stack of old coins at her seat and before mother's, she placed a quilted oven mitt.

"That's for the pie, Mamie," she told my mother so that my mother could place the warm pie down on the table. And I in awe, I watched my mother in full vitality with body and limbs erect and able.

****

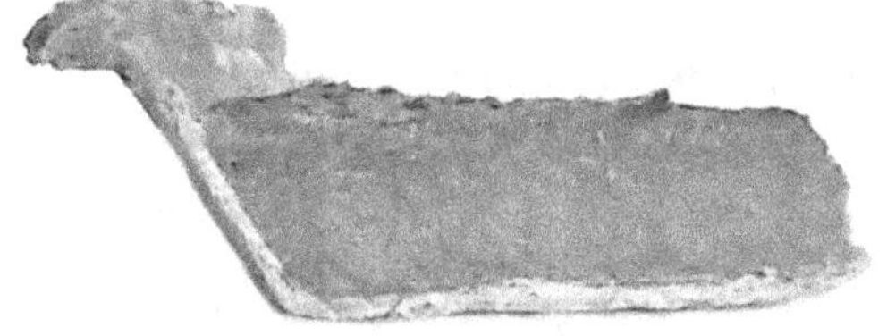

Mother looked and smiled at me indescribably as she placed the warm pie down. It was though she was able to speak to me personally, without ever voicing a sound. "You don't know how long I have been waiting to see your face again!" she expressed this silently through her thoughts. Then humbly I replied, "I am so happy to see you also, mother" although I couldn't express this near enough.

"Now alright you two… Time's a wastin'" Mother and I were humorously told. "Let's not just sit here and let our tea and this pie get cold." This was announced by Aunt Zerita, who being the eldest of the four, often took charge. She was just as lively and loving as ever and still possessed the biggest of hearts.

Following up on her words, Uncle Calvin gently picked up the knife. He was soft-spoken and humble as he ever was, yet so filled with life. "Now give me your plates," he hospitably declared. "I'll do the slicing, so we'll all get our share. As he proceeded to cut, mother began ladling fruit from the bowl. She filled tiny punch cups set next to our tea, which were chilled and still quite cold.

During the laughter and merry interaction as everything was being served, Aunt Minnie sat patiently while she pleasantly observed.

I too took it all in... every moment, every second, every gesture, every laugh and even every expression. For this was sincerely a Godsend – A remarkable blessing.

Oh! And the pie! My goodness yes, the pie! It was incredibly delicious! Briefly after it was served, it all but vanished swiftly from each of our dishes.

From the flaky crust to the light, fluffy filling, each texture was exquisite. Bearing the flavor of authentic ambrosia, this pie definitely confirmed the precise whereabouts of my visit.

****

"This is it! I really am in Heaven!" I zealously thought as I slowly took each precious bite. I was certain that nothing could ever compare to this taste, this moment, my company, as I gladly filled my appetite.

The stories my elders shared as we ate our pie and drank our tea, were filled with such enthralling history and have become such a vital aspect of me.

We wasted not... nor wanted not – Nothing did we crave after everything was finished. Then I noticed, after three doves gracefully flew overhead, the surrounding vivid colors began to fade and diminish. A que it must have been... A subtle signal that it was time to depart. Yet I knew not to let this time of separation weigh heavy on my heart.

"It's only temporary – Us leaving one another" I convinced myself as Mother, Uncle Calvin and Aunt Zerita got up from their seats. Then, they each gave me great hugs and kisses with an 'I love you,' as it was now their time to leave. "You're leaving also?" I asked as Aunt Minnie rose from her chair to join the three. "Yes, little boy" she compassionately confessed, as she too hugged and kissed me.

"I love you, lil ol' boy," she added as she stepped over and in align with her siblings. A mist then began forming around them in the shape of a translucent ring. The ring of mist quickly took the form of a thick cloud around them before their forms disappeared as I did my best, to hold back the tears.

With fulfillment and gratitude, I smiled at them all as the tears welled uncontrollably on the lids of my eyes. Once again, I was bidding farewell to my beloved elders who had all been the love of my life.

****

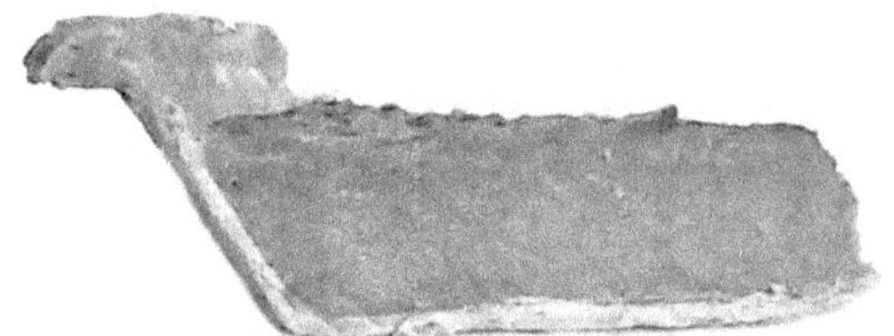

There are no exact words which I might be able to resort to in order to describe this unbelievable experience. All that I know is that I have felt whole and been genuinely blessed ever since. My spirit seems lighter and my mood is less glum. I am even thankful for the littlest of things and all that I have done.

A combination of pure goodness which has been bestowed unto me, exemplifies so much more than merely warm, sweet potato pie accompanied by a nice cup of tea.

From a playful promise I asked Aunt Minnie to keep, long before she had passed... Came a bountiful load of heavenly memories, which I am certain, will forever last.

The End

About the Author

Lord Toph was born and raised in Little Rock Arkansas and attended college at the Memphis College of Art, which once was the Memphis Academy of Art.

He is an artist, author, composer, designer and producer.

He is the founder of Monté CrisToph Multimedia and StarField Stories, a children's literature company. His list of published books include "Heaven, Tea & Sweet Potato Pie," "The Bastard of Indulgence," "Prose for the Unrequited," "Dillinger Comes to Dinner," "Reveries of Romance and Sentiment," "Five Old Wives' Tales," "Poetry for Yoonsil," "Lou Says… Who Says?," "The Girl Who Could Not Sneeze," "Marvin in the Kooky Spooky House," "The Sweet Eaters," "Crusty Bigglebones" and "Fuzzy McKenzie."

Lord Toph has written numerous books and excerpts, some of which remain unpublished.

He currently resides in New York City.

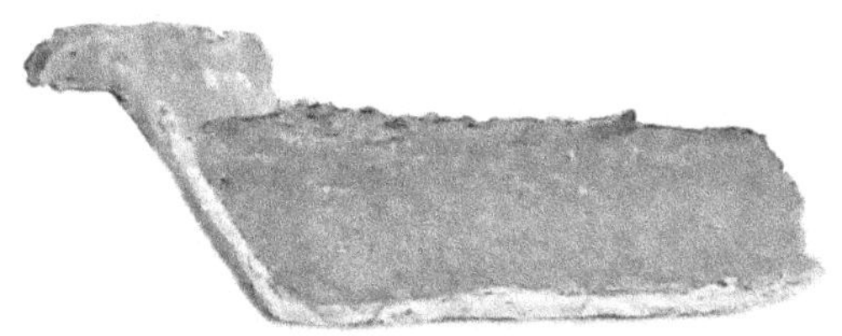

Thank you for reading

"Heaven, Tea & Sweet Potato Pie."

If you have enjoyed the book, please take a moment to provide a positive review to support the author's creative works.

We'd love to hear from you!

Feel free to email us at themanor@montecristoph.com for any feedback or questions.

www.montecristoph.com

"Heaven, Tea & Sweet Potato Pie"

Monté CrisToph Literature

Monté CrisToph Multimedia, Inc.

www.montecristoph.com   themanor@montecristoph.com

www.ingramcontent.com/pod-product-compliance
Lightning Source LLC
LaVergne TN
LVHW020101190726
843498LV00012B/1923